Mere Moments: A Story of Pearl Harbor

The Day the Towers Fell

Two Historical Fiction Stories About America Under Attack

by Amanda Jenkins
illustrated by Larry Johnson

Table of Contents

Focus on the Genre: Historical Fiction 2

Tools for Readers and Writers 4

About the Attacks: Pearl Harbor and
the World Trade Center 5

Mere Moments: A Story of Pearl Harbor 8

The Day the Towers Fell 18

The Writer's Craft: Historical Fiction. 30

Glossary. 32

Make Connections Across Texts. . . Inside Back Cover

HISTORICAL FICTION

What is historical fiction?

Historical fiction stories take place in the past. Historical fiction stories have characters, settings, and events based on historical facts. The characters can be based on real people or made up. The dialogue is made up. But the information about the time period must be authentic, or factually accurate. The stories explore a conflict, or problem, that a character has with himself, with other characters, or with nature.

What is the purpose of historical fiction?

Historical fiction blends history and fiction into stories that could have actually happened. It adds a human element to history. Readers can learn about the time period: how people lived, what they owned, and even what they ate and wore. Readers can also see how people's problems and feelings have not changed much over time. In addition, historical fiction entertains us as we "escape" into adventures from the past.

How do you read historical fiction?

The title gives you a clue about an important time, place, character, or situation. As you read, note how the characters' lives are the same as and different from people's lives today. Note the main characters' thoughts, feelings, and actions. How do they change from the beginning of the story to the end? Ask yourself, *What moves this character to take action? What can I learn today from his or her struggles long ago?*

Features of Historical Fiction

- The characters lived or could have lived in the time and place portrayed.

- The story takes place in an authentic historical setting.

- The events occurred or could have occurred in the setting.

- The dialogue is made up but may be based on letters, a diary, or a report.

- At least one character deals with a conflict (self, others, or nature).

- The story is told from a first-person or third-person point of view.

Who tells the story in historical fiction?

Authors usually write historical fiction in one of two ways. In the first-person point of view, one of the characters tells the story as it happens to him or her, using words such as **I**, **me**, **my**, **mine**, **we**, **us**, and **our**. In the third-person point of view, a narrator tells the story and refers to the characters using words such as **he**, **him**, and **his**; **she**, **her**, and **hers**; and **their**. The narrator may also refer to the characters by name, for example, "Jimmy knew he had no choice but to swim for shore."

Tools for Readers and Writers

Mood

Let's say you've just read the first few pages of a mystery. The setting is a spooky house at the end of a long road. Bare trees blow in the wind as wispy clouds float across the full moon. Animals—you don't know what kind— howl in the distance. All of these descriptions set a creepy, suspenseful mood. Authors want their readers to feel something as they read. That feeling, called mood, may be fear, anger, joy, sadness, and more. When you write, think about what *you* want your readers to feel.

Easily Confused Words

Do you know the difference between **affect** and **effect**? These words are easily confused because they sound similar and have similar spellings—and both can be used as verbs or nouns. They even have similar meanings. Writers can make mistakes, too, and should consult a dictionary when they are confused about the word they want to use.

Sequence of Events

All stories have a beginning, middle, and end. Good authors place events within these three sections so that they build to a final climax. Authors may include key words and phrases to distinguish a sequence of events such as a date, **tonight**, **tomorrow**, **finally**, **after**, and **before**. When writing, make sure to include key events that drive the plot. Readers will better understand the story and want to read more of your works.

About the Attacks

Pearl Harbor, December 7, 1941

By December 1941, Europe had been at war for more than two years. The United States had managed to stay neutral. But U.S. relations with Japan were growing strained. Japan had been expanding its empire by invading other countries. It saw the U.S. as a threat.

On Sunday, December 7, 1941, Japan launched a surprise attack on the U.S. The target: Pearl Harbor, Hawaii—the base for the entire Pacific Naval Fleet. The goal: to cripple the fleet before the U.S. went to war.

At 7:55 A.M., Japanese airplanes and submarines began to bomb ships anchored in the harbor. They also struck air bases and other military installations. By 10:00 A.M., the attack was over. Eighteen American ships had been sunk or severely damaged. A total of 188 aircraft had been destroyed, and 3,500 Americans had been killed or wounded.

The next day, the U.S. declared war on Japan. On December 11, Japan's allies Germany and Italy declared war on the U.S. America had officially entered World War II.

The World Trade Center, September 11, 2001

On the morning of September 11, 2001, terrorists attacked the United States. Armed men pretending to be regular passengers boarded four different airplanes. They hijacked the planes in mid-flight and crashed them into their chosen targets.

Two planes rammed into the quarter-mile-tall World Trade Center towers in New York City. Everyone onboard the planes died instantly. As the towers burned, rescue workers rushed to help. People who had been inside began to make their way out. Both buildings collapsed before everyone could escape. The towers' fall was so violent that it destroyed more buildings nearby.

The third hijacked plane headed toward Washington, D.C. It crashed into the Pentagon, the headquarters for the U.S. military. Everyone on the airplane was killed, along with some people inside the building.

Passengers on the fourth airplane learned what had happened to the other three planes. They chose to fight back. The passengers tried to regain control of the aircraft, but the hijackers put the plane into a nosedive. United Airlines Flight 93 crashed into a field in Pennsylvania, killing everyone onboard.

More than 3,000 people of all nationalities, races, and religions died in the 9/11 attacks.

8:46	9:03	9:59	10:28
NORTH TOWER HIT	SOUTH TOWER HIT	SOUTH TOWER COLLAPSE	NORTH TOWER COLLAPSE

Mere Moments:
A Story of Pearl Harbor

D o it now! Jimmy urged himself. *Ask her!*
It was the perfect time and place for a marriage proposal: a clear, star-filled evening with the scent of gardenias and hibiscus on the breeze. Though early December, it was surprisingly balmy, even for Hawaii. Jimmy was on shore leave from his ship, the USS *Utah*, and he and Doreen were outside under a string of swaying lanterns, dancing to music from a supper club's band.

Romance was certainly in the air, but Jimmy was so nervous that he kept stepping on Doreen's feet. The engagement ring in its box was a heavy lump in the pocket of his navy uniform pants. He hoped that the sweat from his palm wasn't seeping through the back of Doreen's dress.

He'd known that Doreen was the girl for him the first time he'd met her just six weeks ago, on the beach at Waikiki. He'd been sure she felt the same way about him . . . until now. Now he was worried she might say no.

Really, Doreen was too good for him. She resembled movie star Rita Hayworth, whose picture was pinned in many of the sailors' lockers. And not only was Doreen beautiful, she was smart and independent, a nurse at the Naval Hospital.

Females were few and far between at Pearl Harbor. Doreen could have any guy she wanted: a doctor, an officer, a pilot from the Naval Air Station. Why would she ever want a guy like Jimmy? A lowly seaman second class wasn't very impressive compared to an ace pilot who could **flaunt** his flying skills to impress the ladies.

The song, "Take the A Train," ended. Jimmy let go of Doreen and tried to discreetly wipe his damp palms on his pants.

"Are you all right?" Doreen asked as they walked back to their table. "You're awfully quiet."

"I'm fine," Jimmy told her, though his chest tightened. Maybe this wasn't the right time for a proposal after all. He'd agreed to see Doreen tomorrow morning at church; maybe he'd feel more like proposing then.

Tonight's shore leave ended at midnight, and as usual Jimmy fought the urge to **flout** orders by staying out late with Doreen. He made it back aboard the *Utah* with only moments to spare.

Unlike the *Arizona* or the *Oklahoma* or the *Raleigh*—or most of the other vessels currently anchored at Pearl Harbor—the *Utah* was no longer a fighting ship. She had been refitted to serve as a mobile target so that aviators could practice dropping bombs on her. The practice bombs were inert and couldn't explode, but they could still penetrate the *Utah*'s steel deck, which was covered with thick six-by-twelve wooden timbers for training sessions.

Aboard ship, Jimmy glumly stowed the box containing Doreen's engagement ring in his locker. *I'll propose tomorrow*, he told himself as he climbed into his bunk.

The next morning he wasn't quite so sure. He thought about the ring as he got dressed. Today didn't seem like the right time, either. *I'll ask her next week*, he decided as he bent to tie his shoes. *Or maybe at Christmas. Or maybe on New Year's Eve . . . that would be romantic!*

BOOM!!! An explosion shook the ship, knocking Jimmy to the floor.

Explosions weren't anything new to the *Utah*—but right now she was in harbor, not at sea! What was going on? As Jimmy got to his feet, dazed and **nonplussed**, all he could think was that some fool was using the ship for torpedo practice while she was still in port.

I'm going to use him for target practice, thought Jimmy.

Someone shouted, "The Japanese are attacking!"

The Japanese?

The *Utah* had begun to tip toward her port side. She shuddered as another torpedo hit.

BOOM!

This was no drill! Jimmy joined the rush to battle quarters.

Mere minutes had **passed** since the first hit, but it was already clear that the *Utah* was capsizing. Her decks slanted more and more steeply every second. Jimmy barely had time to reach his assigned station on the third deck below when the order came to abandon ship.

Everyone began scrambling back up the ladders to the main deck.

The escaping crew—including Jimmy—emerged to a deafening thunder of explosions, plane engines, and machine-gun fire. The Hawaiian sky, normally an inviting blue, was filled with smoke from burning ships. Japanese airplanes darted and circled overhead, dropping bombs and then swooping to rake the anchored ships with gunfire.

The *Utah's* anti-aircraft guns were still inside their thick steel casings. Even if there had been time for her crew to fight back, there was no way to do so.

Rat-a-tat-tat-tat-tat! Machine-gun fire came from the *Raleigh*, anchored nearby. Some of the U.S. ships were still able to shoot at the attacking planes!

Jimmy heard cheers. "Get 'em, boys!" someone shouted.

"Move it!" A sailor pushed his way past Jimmy. "Let me off this sinking tub!"

He joined other men swarming down the tilted deck to the port side of the ship. Since it was already underwater, they stepped easily into the sea and began to swim. But the *Utah* was at such at a crazy angle that her heavy protective timbers were coming loose. A couple rolled past Jimmy, thudding and bumping.

"Look out!" someone shouted, but it was too late. Men screamed as the timbers smashed into their legs and sent them careening down the oil-slicked deck.

Splash! The thick timbers hit the water. The men who had been swimming there disappeared beneath them.

The only way to go was up. Jimmy climbed the angled deck to starboard until he was high in the air, standing on the *Utah*'s exposed side. Her waterline was marked with a thick line of slimy oil. Spilling fuel from the damaged ships spread over the ocean's surface in a sludgy, **flammable** slick; the water itself would start to burn as soon as fire touched it.

Jimmy knew he had no choice but to swim for shore, but first he had to somehow make his way down a sloping hull crusted with razor-sharp barnacles. As he hesitated, there was a loud strafing hail of bullets and something smacked into him—it felt as if he'd been punched in the gut—and the next thing he knew, he was sliding down the ship's hull toward the water, barnacles shredding his pants and slicing his legs all the way down.

Then he was underwater. One startled moment later he began to kick. He paddled his way to the surface where he gulped in a deep breath of air as well as a mouthful of oily seawater.

To his horror, he was now covered in the same **inflammable** fuel oil that slicked the water. One spark would set him ablaze.

I've got to get out of here, Jimmy thought.

All around, other men were in the water, too, all coated in the same black gunk. Some bobbed facedown, already dead. Others were trying to get to the beach hundreds of feet away.

Jimmy struck out for shore. It was the longest swim of his life.

Screeeeeeee! Bombs shrieked as they fell. *Ka-BOOM!* Geysers of water shot upward with each explosion. *Vroooooooom!* Airplanes dove down, coming closer and closer.

Tat-tat-tat-tat-tat! Japanese planes peppered the men in the sea with machine-gun fire. When a guy got hit, his arms would go up and he'd sink beneath the waves.

It seemed like forever before Jimmy felt his feet touch solid ground.

As he dragged himself out of the water, he saw other men running for the safety of a trench along the shoreline. He tried to run with them, but instead he collapsed in the sand. He was surprised to see blood pooling beside him. He stared at it in wonder as everything went dark.

***

When he opened his eyes he was looking at a white ceiling and the face of a girl who resembled Rita Hayworth. Jimmy blinked, confused. "Doreen?" She was wearing her nurse's uniform.

"Shh," said Doreen. "Don't try to talk. You're in the hospital. You've been shot."

Jimmy remembered the blood in the sand and his feeling of being punched in the gut. Had that been a bullet?

"You're going to be all right." Doreen looked exhausted but her voice was steady. "No, don't talk," she said again, as Jimmy tried to speak. "I just wanted you to know you're going to be okay."

Now Jimmy saw that her uniform had spots of blood on it. Now he heard the sounds around him: groans, cries for water, voices murmuring orders.

Doreen's eyes were puffy with dark circles under them. Had she been working around the clock?

"I can't stay," Doreen told him. "The hospital's overflowing with wounded and there are hundreds of men needing help." She bent to give Jimmy a kiss on the cheek. "I love you. I'll be back when I can," she added and then turned to go.

I love you? She loves me?

This was the time. Now. There might not be another.

"Doreen?" Jimmy called weakly, and when she glanced back he asked, "Marry me?"

"Of course," Doreen said matter-of-factly and gave him a smile.

Then she was gone.

Jimmy lay back and closed his eyes. It didn't matter that the engagement ring was lost. The ring didn't matter at all anymore. The *Utah*—and other ships, Jimmy didn't yet know how many— lay under the waters of Pearl Harbor, with some of their crews forever inside.

War had begun. If it wasn't official yet, it would be soon.

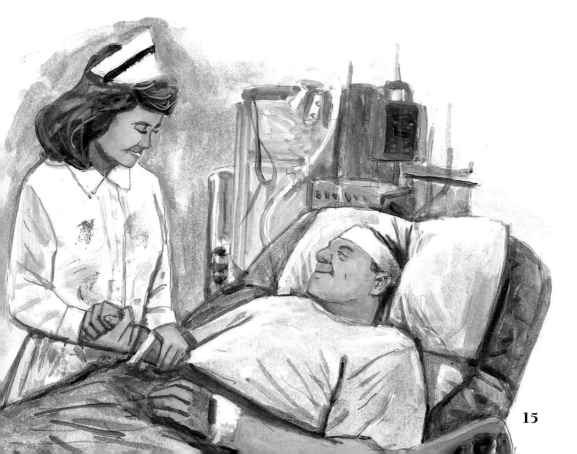

Analyze the Characters, Setting, and Plot

- Who are the characters in the story?
- Where and when does the story take place?
- What problem do the characters face?
- What major events occur in the story?
- How does the time period affect the characters' problem?
- How is the problem solved?

Focus on Comprehension:
Sequence of Events

- What happens to the *Utah* right after she is hit by torpedoes?
- What does Jimmy think right after the torpedoes hit?
- What does Jimmy need to do before he can swim ashore?
- What happens right after Jimmy makes it to shore?

Focus on Simultaneous Events

Sometimes events in a story happen simultaneously, or at the exact same time. This story has many simultaneous events, including the events on the ship after it was hit and the events occurring in the water as men were trying to swim to safety. Choose one time and describe the events.

Analyze the Tools Writers Use: Mood

- What is the mood for the first part of the story at the dance?
- The middle part of the story is about the attack on Pearl Harbor. The author includes many moods including fear and desperation. Choose one mood and provide evidence that supports your choice.
- Reread the final part of the story where Jimmy and Doreen are in the hospital. This section has a mixed mood. Identify two moods. Why do you think the author ended the story this way?

Focus on Words: Easily Confused Words

Locate the easily confused words in the story. Read the sentence containing the word and the sentences around it. Make a chart like the one below. Then write a definition for the word. Finally, identify clue words from the text that helped you determine the meaning of the easily confused word.

Page	Word	Definition	Clue Words That Helped You Determine Word Meaning
9	flaunt		
10	flout		
11	nonplussed		
11	passed		
13	flammable		
13	inflammable		

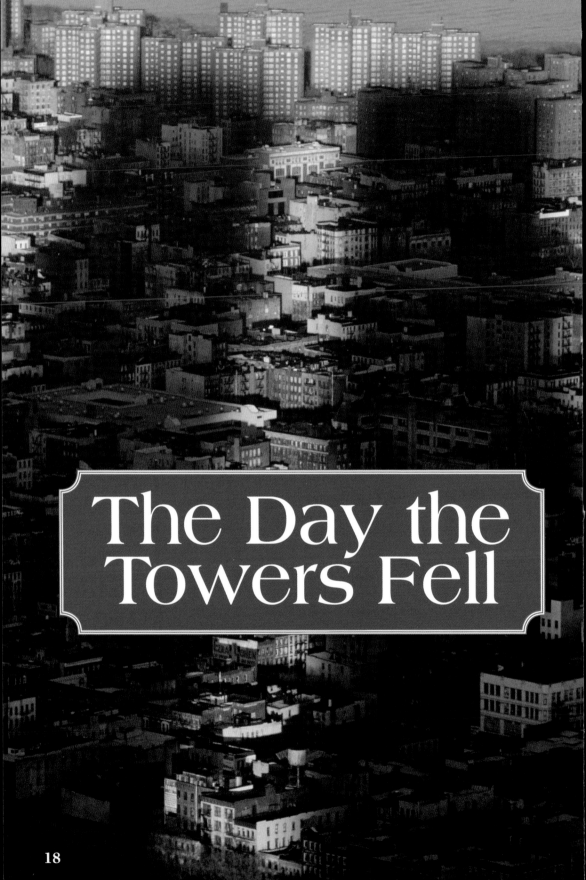

The Day the Towers Fell

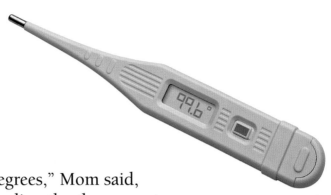

99.6

degrees," Mom said, reading the thermometer she'd just pulled out of my mouth. "Your fever is down but not gone." Awesome! I was going to miss school for the second **consecutive** day!

I admit that I wasn't feeling that sick, but I **lay** in bed trying to look pathetic. The last time I'd stayed home from school, I was nine and afraid to be alone in our New York City apartment. Now I was fourteen, a freshman in high school—and having a day to myself sounded pretty good to me!

Mom **laid** the thermometer on the nightstand, looking thoughtful. She'd missed work yesterday to stay with me; she couldn't afford to miss another day and had to leave soon so she wouldn't be late. She always took the subway from our apartment in Chelsea to her receptionist job in the Financial District.

Mom fixed me with her behave-yourself-young-man stare. "I know you're feeling better, Aaron," she warned, "but when I say rest, I mean it."

"Yes, ma'am," I said. I never could fool my mother.

"And if you get scared while I'm at work—"

"Come on, Mom," I interrupted, "I can handle it!"

> The author establishes the setting and age of the main character. The story is being told in the first-person point of view.

> The author gives more details about the setting, which is a key part of the story.

"Okay. I'm just saying that if you need help, call Mrs. Malik."

I suppressed a snicker. Mrs. Malik was the elderly Bengali woman who lived in the apartment next door. I liked her, but it was hilarious to think that she could ever help me. She had to be at least seventy years old; **besides**, she needed a walker to get around—the kind with tennis balls stuck on the ends of the legs to help it slide better!

Before Mom left for work, she opened the blinds in my room. Our apartment was tiny, but my window had a great view southward: a broad, sturdy landscape of rooftops, chimneys, and tall buildings.

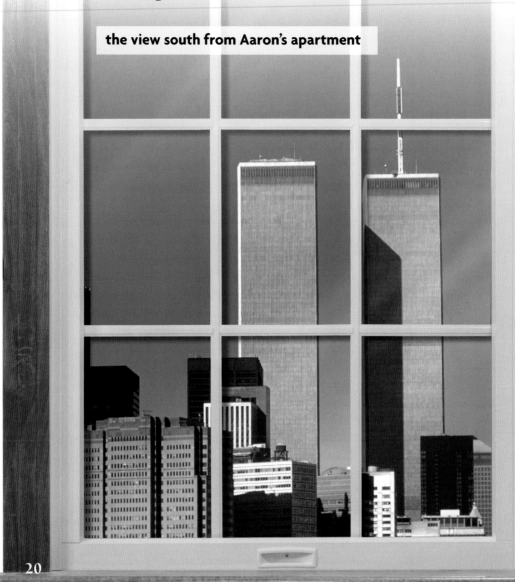

the view south from Aaron's apartment

Tallest of all were the Twin Towers of the World Trade Center where my mom worked, two solid glass-and-steel anchors that pinned the skyline down.

Today the sky above them was clear, cloudless, and bright blue. Tuesday, September 11, 2001: a perfect day to stay home from school. I stretched out under the covers, lazy and relaxed, luxuriating in the knowledge that I didn't have to get up until I felt like it.

I had **lain** in bed for a couple of hours before I rolled sleepily to sit up. I didn't bother to glance out the window, just checked the clock—it was almost ten—and ambled into the living room. I found the remote, flopped onto the sofa, and turned on the television. There was some movie on about a burning skyscraper, but I flipped **past** it, fingers skimming automatically to hit the buttons that took me to video games.

Except . . . wait a minute. Was that a movie? It looked like it might be a news program. I went back to check.

The scene leaped off the screen and punched me in the gut.

Fire. Smoke. Glass. Steel. The World Trade Center. Where my mom was. Right this minute.

". . . two commercial airliners have flown into the Twin Towers," the newscaster was saying. "A roof rescue is not possible because of the intense heat and smoke . . ."

I got up so fast that I hit my shin on the coffee table. Tripping over my own feet, I stumbled to my bedroom and looked out the window again.

It was real. All of it.

The author introduces the historical event that is the basis of the story: the day the Twin Towers fell. She researched details about that day, such as the weather in NYC.

The author introduces the problem of the story. Aaron is home, watching TV reports of the World Trade Center attack, while his mother is in the middle of it. This information sends him into emotional turmoil (confusion and agitation). A character in turmoil leads to compelling stories that captivate readers.

The burning towers jutted into the sky. Each had a black gash in its side, as if a bite had been taken out of it. Dark, ferocious smoke poured out of the gashes, boiling upward.

Mom's office was on the thirty-first floor of the North Tower.

I raced to the phone in the kitchen. I couldn't think straight and my fingers fumbled, hitting the wrong buttons twice before I finally managed to dial my mother's cell.

Brrrrrrring. Brrrrrrring.

"Come on, Mom, pick up," I whispered hoarsely, making my way back to the window.

Brrrrrrring. Brrrrrrring.

Outside, the top of the South Tower—the part above the burning gash—tilted slightly, drooping. Then it dropped. And kept dropping.

In one long and terrible moment, the building collapsed downward, each floor gobbling the one beneath.

Where the South Tower had been, there was now only empty space and a thick, ugly column of smoke. The skyline was raw and broken. One of its anchors was gone.

The phone fell from my hand. How many people had been inside? How many had died in that long and terrible moment? Hundreds? Thousands? Tens of thousands?

The front doorbell rang.

"Mom!" I scrambled into the living room and flung the door open. Mrs. Malik peered up at me from the hallway.

"I just came to see how you . . . ."

I don't know what my face looked like, but I could feel that my cheeks were wet, so I swiped the back of my hand across my eyes.

Mrs. Malik's jaw set tight. The next thing I knew she was bustling around the apartment, telling me to get cups out while she made us some tea.

"Don't you worry, Aaron," she assured me as she put water on to boil. "I'm sure your mother's on her way home. She probably had to take the stairs to get out of the building, and it took her a while to walk down all those steps. You're not supposed to use an elevator during a fire, you know."

I realized she was right. Most elevators have signs in them that say, "In case of fire, use stairs."

The author moves the story along by bringing in Mrs. Malik, who turns out to be considerably more capable than Aaron had thought. The author also makes the problem worse. Aaron can't communicate with his mother, which makes him (and the readers) even more worried.

"I tried to call her, but she didn't answer."

"I just tried to call you, and there was no answer—that's why I came over. The phone systems are erratic right now, and I've heard that most of the subways aren't running, either. Your mother may have to walk home, and I'm going to stay with you until she gets here. Now, help me find two spoons."

When the tea was ready, I carried it into the living room and sat on the sofa with Mrs. Malik. I didn't like tea and was too freaked out to drink any even if I'd wanted to, but something about holding the warm cup and cradling it in my hands seemed to steady me.

We watched and listened to the news. When a reporter said, "It was a terrorist attack, no two ways about it," Mrs. Malik seemed to crumple a little.

When I saw her suddenly looking frail and feeble again, I realized that it wasn't the tea steadying me. It was having someone **beside** me when things seemed bleak. It was knowing that I wasn't alone.

Before today, I never would have thought I'd hold a little old lady's hand—but now I found myself doing just that.

Brrrrrrrring!

I pounced on the phone. "Mom? Hello? Mom?"

"Aaron?" It was Mom. I sagged with relief. "I've been trying and trying to get through," I heard her say. "Are you all right?"

"Me?" I couldn't believe she was asking that; I was the one who'd been safe at home the whole time. "I'm fine. Are you all right? Where are you?"

"I'm in the lobby of a bank. I'm okay. I'm on my way home."

We didn't talk long because the connection was bad, but it didn't matter. My mother was safe!

After we hung up, I went back to sit with Mrs. Malik. I knew she still needed me.

The author has the main character show heartfelt emotions, a contrast to his brasher attitude earlier in the story. This also shows his growth as a character.

Aaron responds to the good news that his mother is alive by sagging with relief. Authors use strong, vivid verbs to describe actions, show characters' feelings, and express mood.

All that morning, Mrs. Malik and I stayed together. Together we watched the North Tower fall. Together we learned that there had been four **concurrent** hijackings; a third airplane had crashed into the Pentagon, and a fourth went down in a field in Pennsylvania. The passengers had banded together to prevent yet another attack, giving their own lives in the process.

The author includes additional factual information from 9/11/01. Historical fiction is a blend of fiction and fact.

When my mom finally made it home, she was exhausted, bedraggled, and covered in white dust. Her hands and knees were bandaged. She cried as I hugged her.

Mrs. Malik made more tea while Mom told us what had happened.

"I never made it to work today. I was late, taking care of Aaron, and I was two blocks away when the North Tower was hit," she said. "I heard a terrible roar, and everyone around me started screaming and running. I looked back to see a tidal wave of ash and dust and debris coming down the street—and I started running, too. In the panic I tripped and fell, but I managed to get up and duck into the nearest doorway just as the debris cloud hit."

Mom's hands were shaking so hard that she had to set her cup down. "Everything went dark," she continued, "as if night had fallen. The air was so thick that it was hard to breathe. I don't know how long I crouched there, huddling with people I'd never met before. All their faces were blank with shock and terror. I know mine was, too, because I felt the same way."

Mom looked down at her bandaged hands. "I didn't even know I was injured until I'd started home again. When I fell, I must have landed on broken glass, but I didn't feel it, and I didn't notice I was bleeding until some lady came up to me on the street and told me I was hurt. She drew me aside and hugged me and cleaned my wounds and bandaged them."

Mom's eyes filled with tears again. "All the way home people—strangers—kept asking if I needed help. On every single block, people—strangers—were in the street giving away bottles of water, giving directions to anyone who was lost, giving help to anyone who was injured or needed to rest. Strangers no more."

September 11, 2001, was the worst day of my life, but also, in some ways, one of the best.

The author has the character of Aaron's mother tell how she managed to survive the tragedy. Although the event was harrowing, and readers may feel disturbed by it, the story also shows that a crisis situation often brings out the best in people. Like Aaron and his mother, readers may feel ennobled by the compassionate actions of the people on the streets.

Analyze the Characters, Setting, and Plot

- Who are the characters in the story?
- Where and when does the story take place?
- What problems do the characters face?
- What major events occur in the story?
- How does the time period affect the characters' problem? Or doesn't it? Explain.
- How is the problem solved?

Focus on Comprehension: Sequence of Events

- What does Aaron do right after he flips past the burning skyscraper on the TV?
- What has Mrs. Malik done right before she goes to Aaron's house?
- What does Aaron do right after his mom calls home?

Analyze the Tools Writers Use: Mood

- What is the mood for the part of the story when Aaron first realizes the Trade Center towers have been hit?
- When Mrs. Malik arrives to stay with Aaron, the author transitions into a different mood. Aaron is still very scared, but Mrs. Malik calms him by keeping him busy. How would you describe the mood of the story at this point?
- Aaron's mother describes what happened to her as she tried to get home. What words does the author use to create a mood of desperation and fear?

Focus on Words:
Easily Confused Words

Locate the easily confused words in the story. Read the sentence containing the word and the sentences around it. Make a chart like the one below. Then write a definition for the word. Finally, identify clue words from the text that helped you determine the meaning of the easily confused word.

Page	Word	Definition	Clue Words That Helped You Determine Word Meaning
19	consecutive		
19	lay		
19	laid		
20	besides		
21	lain		
21	past		
25	beside		
26	concurrent		

How does an author write
HISTORICAL FICTION?

Reread "The Day the Towers Fell" and think about what Amanda Jenkins did to write this story. How did she develop the story? How can you, as a writer, develop your own historical fiction?

1.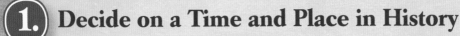

Decide on a Time and Place in History

a. Choose a time 30 years ago, 3,000 years ago, or somewhere in between. Set your story in your home country or far away.

b. Learn everything you can about the lives of people who lived in that time and place so your story details will be authentic. In "The Day the Towers Fell," the author researched the 9/11 attacks in NYC and interviewed people who lived through it.

c. Choose an actual event to rewrite into your own historical fiction story, or create a story based on the life of a historical figure.

Character	Traits	Examples
Aaron	brash; worried; upset; thankful	thinks he will have an easy day off from school and sleeps late; concerned when he realizes that his mother works in the World Trade Center, the buildings that are under attack; is crying when Mrs. Malik opens the door; very relieved when he hears his mother on the phone
Mrs. Malik	physically frail; mentally tough; dependable	needs a walker to get around, but takes charge when she goes to see Aaron (makes tea, sits with him)
Aaron's mother	caring; responsible; resourceful; brave; appreciative	she stays home to take care of Aaron the first day he is sick but goes to work on the second day; takes shelter in a bank during the attack; walks home in the aftermath, injured; tells about all the giving people who offered help to her (and to others) on her walk home

Brainstorm Characters

Writers ask these questions:

- What kind of person will my main character be?
  What are his or her traits, or qualities?
- What things are important to my main character? What does
  he or she want?
- What other characters will be important to my story?
  How will each character help or hinder the main character?
- How will the characters change? What will they learn about life?

Brainstorm Plot

Writers ask these questions:

- What are some important incidents that actually occurred in my historical
  setting? How can I turn one of those real-life experiences into a story?
- What is the problem, or situation?
- What events happen?
- How does the story end?
- Will my readers be entertained? Will they learn something?

Setting	Aaron's apartment and the streets of lower Manhattan, September 11, 2001
Problem of the Story	Aaron thinks his mother is at work in the World Trade Center when the towers are attacked.
Story Events	1. Aaron, age fourteen, is sick and staying home from school. 2. Aaron's mother goes to work but tells Aaron that the elderly Mrs. Malik next door will look in on him (which Aaron thinks is unnecessary). 3. Aaron naps a bit, wakes up, turns on the TV, and realizes that the World Trade Center is under attack. 4. He can't get through to his mother on the phone and becomes increasingly worried. 5. Mrs. Malik comes over and helps calm Aaron with tea and her company. They continue to watch the horrible events unfold on TV.
Solution to the Problem	Aaron's mother finally gets through on the phone and assures Aaron she is okay. When she comes home a bit later, she tells how she escaped the attack and was helped by strangers during the long walk home.

Glossary

beside (bih-SIDE) next to (page 25)

besides (bih-SIDEZ) together with (page 20)

concurrent (kun-KER-ent) happening at the same time (page 26)

consecutive (kun-SEH-kyuh-tiv) following one after the other in order (page 19)

flammable (FLA-muh-bul) capable of easily catching fire (page 13)

flaunt (FLAUNT) display brazenly (page 9)

flout (FLOWT) to treat with disregard; scorn (page 10)

inflammable (in-FLA-muh-bul) capable of easily catching fire (page 13)

laid (LADE) placed (page 19)

lain (LANE) reclined (page 21)

lay (LAY) to place for rest or sleep (page 19)

nonplussed (nahn-PLUST) puzzled; perplexed (page 11)

passed (PAST) happened; occurred (page 11)

past (PAST) beyond (page 21)